To Wanda and Rosie,
who are great friends to play with
and usually behave at dinner!
Neil x

To my dino friends Mo, Zaley, Gavin,
Linden, Charlotte, Matthew and Ryan.
You can come to dinner anytime!
Peggy x

Red Robin
BOOKS
Where story matters

Red Robin Books is an imprint of Corner To Learn Limited

Published by
Corner To Learn Limited
Willow Cottage • 26 Purton Stoke
Swindon • Wiltshire SN5 4JF • UK

ISBN: 978-1-905434-84-8

First published in the UK 2011
Text © Neil Griffiths 2011
Illustrations © Peggy Collins 2011

The rights of Neil Griffiths to be identified as the
author of this work has been asserted by him in accordance
with the Copyright, Designs and Patents Act 1988.

Design by
David Rose

Printed in China

Don't invite DINOSAURS to dinner

Neil Griffiths

Illustrated by
Peggy Collins

To:
THE
DINOSAURS
(please come to dinner)

MAIL

T. REX
B. SAURUS
P.T. RANADON
S.T. O'SAURUS

Don't invite dinosaurs to **dinner**,
As they're bound to make an awful mess.

Don't even take them out **clothes shopping**,
Unless you want them to rip every dress.

Don't ever take dinosaurs **swimming,**

And if you foolishly take them **sailing**,
Then you've only got yourself to blame.

Don't invite dinosaurs to **football**,
As you'll never have a happy game.

And please don't take them out **camping**,
As you'll end up looking a fool.

As the water
will **GUSH**
from the pool!

Don't take dinosaurs to a **fun fair**,
As there won't be room
on the ride.

As they'll only **terrify** the bride!

And please don't invite them to a **wedding**,

And if you ever
take them ice-skating,

Open

Don't let dinosaurs in a **library**,
As you know they just
won't be QUIET.

Then please put them first on a **diet**.

Don't include dinosaurs in Sports Day,

And don't take them with you to **ballet**,
As the last thing they can do
is dance!

As no-one will stand
an **earthly** chance.

As the ropes will never take the strain.

And if you take them with you on **holiday**,
Promise me it won't be by plane.

Please don't let dinosaurs bungee jump,

Open

Don't invite dinosaurs to your school,
As they just won't fit through the door.

And a visit to a
supermarket,
Will see tins
tumbling
to the floor.

And as for visiting a **ZOO,**

It's just not the place they should be.

And don't take them with you to the **circus,**

As no-one will be
able to see.

But if it's **play time** you are after,
Then it's dinosaurs you should invite.

They are the best of fun
to have as **play pals**,
As they will play from
morning till night.

You will climb up the highest of mountains.

And slip down the **longest** slide.

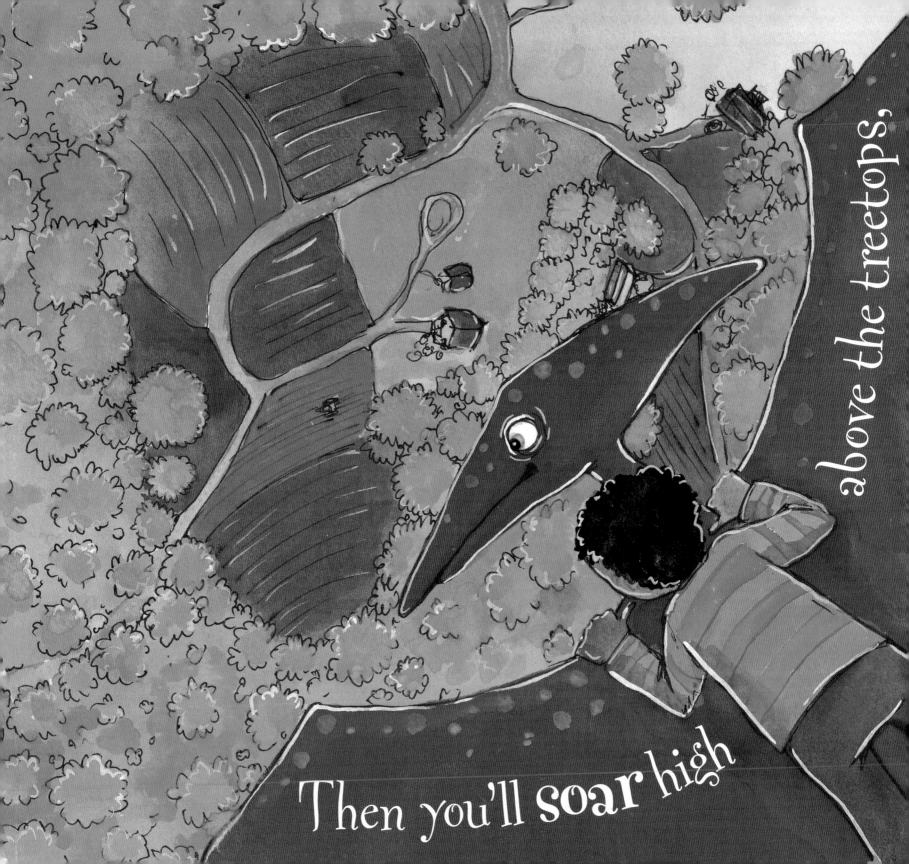

Then you'll soar high above the treetops,

And find the best of places to hide.

And at night time they will **rock** you gently,
Until fast asleep you'll fall.

So yes, **DO** invite dinosaurs over,
As they seem to be
fun after all!